MW01100260

Andrew's Gift

Andrew's Gift

Sharon Coleman

TATE PUBLISHING
AND ENTERPRISES, LLC

Published by Tate Publishing & Enterprises, LLC
127 E. Trade Center Terrace | Mustang, Oklahoma 73064 USA
1.888.361.9473 | www.tatepublishing.com

Tate Publishing is committed to excellence in the publishing industry. The company reflects the philosophy established by the founders, based on Psalm 68:11,
"The Lord gave the word and great was the company of those who published it."

Book design copyright © 2012 by Tate Publishing, LLC. All rights reserved.
Cover design by Blake Brasor
Interior design by Lindsay B. Behrens

Published in the United States of America

ISBN: 978-1-61862-811-4
1. Fiction / Christian / General
2. Fiction / Family Life
12.04.18

To my grandchildren, precious gifts from God.

In the order that you came to me, Caitlyn,
Colten, Austin and Savannah, I love you
to the moon and back…and beyond!

In Loving Memory of
Myrna Mae McLean
On earth: 2-17-1941 – 10-01-2011
In Heaven: 10-01-2011 – forever

Some people give gifts; you were a gift.

…One day Lord You've promised
When I walk through life's final door
I will never have to say good-bye again
Forevermore.

Acknowledgements

All thanks and praise to my Lord and Savior, Jesus Christ, without whom this work would never have come to pass. In Him I truly do live and move and have my being. It is in Him, by Him, and through Him that I am able to do this thing I have loved for so many years—write. He helps me take the experiences of life, good and bad, and mold them into words that, somehow, miraculously speak to the hearts of others. He is amazing!

Thank you to my patient and loving husband, Mike. You put up with me when I have my head in the clouds and my mind miles away from our home on "The Ridge"! You keep me grounded, and your encouragement has been my bread and butter. You are the best husband, dad, and "Poppy" in the world. Thanks for the best thirty-some years of my life.

And to my friends and coworkers at Family Resource Center of Lincoln County (FRC), you are the best! Your encouragement has meant the world to me, and your patience during this process has been a Godsend. What you do is amazing, and your work with victims and the homeless, while largely unnoticed and unappreciated by man, does not go unnoticed by God. He who sees what you do in obscurity will reward you openly! God Bless you, my dear friends.

Simple Gifts

What gift is right to give this child
This newborn King so meek and mild?
An eagerness to serve and please
And worship Him on bended knees

What gift you ask for this young King
Will He accept our offering?

He has no need of gold or fame
Nor does he look for earthly gain
He came to give Himself you see
God's perfect gift to you and me

What gift can we to Him impart?
The simple gift of a child's heart

"…Receive the Kingdom of God like a child…"

Luke 18:17

One

Mary awoke to see that darkness still reigned outside her bedroom window. Morning used to be her favorite part of the day, but not anymore. Now every time she opened her eyes, she relived that awful moment all over again. Nine months had passed since she answered her door to a man in uniform with news that had forever changed her world. Mary wondered if she would ever again feel the oblivion of sleep lift without the stabbing awareness of dread and sorrow.

She had heard somewhere that the first year of mourning was the worst because of all of the "firsts" it entailed. There was the first birthday without him, first anniversary without him, first Thanksgiving without him, and now the first Christmas without him.

Andrew always loved the Christmas Season and all that it entailed. He loved picking out and decorating a tree, and he loved adorning the house with Christmas lights, inside and out. His gifts of choice were usually imaginative and well thought out. Last minute shopping was reserved for last minute gifts. She was much more inclined to do last minute shopping than he. Once the children began to arrive, Christmas Eve would usually find him up all night finishing a hand made gift or assembling a toy of some kind.

But Iraq had changed all of that forever. It was supposed to be his last deployment, and so it had been. He had died as he had lived, giving his all to those around him. She was proud of him, but the medals on her dresser couldn't wrap her in a hug; they wouldn't wait up with her when the time came for their daughters' first dates, and they wouldn't teach their son how to respect a girl or pitch a baseball.

By the light of the streetlamp outside, Mary could see that it had begun to snow. At least the children would have a white Christmas, she thought. Her mind wandered to a list of things she needed to do that day. The Christmas party preparations would dominate her day, and perhaps staying busy would keep her from thinking too much about Andrew...

She closed her eyes and whispered the prayer that had become her daily mantra. "Lord, I need your grace to make it today. Please prepare my way before me, and equip me for whatever You bring my way. I ask these things in Your precious name Lord, Amen."

Baby steps, she told herself. I need to make it through this day. Then I need to make it through the rest of the holiday season. Then with the New Year, maybe she and the children could begin to put the pieces of their lives back together. One day at a time, she reminded herself, one day at a time. And with that she took a deep breath, slowly exhaled, and resolutely rolled out of bed.

Two

Mary completed the final touches to the mantel and stepped back to view her work. The large room was resplendent with Christmas glamour. The huge tree dominating the bay window was still not large enough to shelter all of the packages that crowded beneath it and spilled out to claim the surrounding area as well.

"A lot of presents for one child," she mused to herself.

Satisfied that all was perfection, she retreated to the kitchen to insure that the caterers were progressing on schedule with the party preparations. She then ran upstairs one more time to check on the nanny and five-year-old Jack. It simply wouldn't do for the child to interrupt the party, not with all of the important guests that were expected.

Mary looked at her watch. She couldn't wait any longer. She walked slowly down the stairs and to the back hallway where she retrieved her coat. As she did, she heard the brisk *clip-clip* of heels on the polished granite floors. She turned her attention to the striking young woman approaching. Clothed and coiffed to perfection, she wore a satisfied expression on her flawless features.

"Mary, you've done it again! Whatever would we do without you! As we discussed, you may have tomorrow off, but I will need you here bright and early the day after to help me prepare for my women's group. Now, run along, and, oh yes, Merry Christmas."

As she said this, she held out an envelope. "Here is your paycheck. I know I promised you a bonus for Christmas, but with so much on my mind, I completely forgot when I wrote your check. I'm sure you already have your Christmas planned and prepared anyway. You are so good at that! Let's just say that having the day off is your bonus, okay? I know for us, doing without you tomorrow is more of a sacrifice than money! But we will muddle through somehow. Don't you worry about us." With that, she turned and *clip-clipped* back through the hallway into the brightly lit living room beyond.

Mary swallowed her tears of disappointment. She had counted on that bonus along with last-minute department store sales to purchase a few presents for her children. She didn't know what she was going to do. She had to use her paycheck to pay her rent and utilities, and to purchase a few groceries. There would be no more than pennies left once those obligations were met. Slowly, she donned her thin coat and scarf and walked to the bus stop. As she did, she prayed for wisdom and provision.

Three

Mary closed her eyes against the bright Christmas lights that seemed to mock her as they swirled passed the bus window. Her eyes burning with unshed tears, she allowed her mind to drift.

Oh, Andrew, how I miss you! I know all things work together for good for those who are called according to God's purposes, but I am having a hard time seeing any purpose or good right now! I am so proud of you for serving our county and for leaving such an inspiring legacy to our children, but we miss you so much! We miss the 'us' that we used to be! Nothing is the same without you. I don't know what to do right now, and I need you to help me, but you're not here!

In the depth of her anguished soul, she heard a whisper, *Come, all you who are burdened and heavy laden for I will give you rest!*

Thirty minutes later, as she walked the two blocks home from the bus stop, Mary grappled with what she would tell her children. She was thankful for the few handmade items she had been able to complete for them. Those were going to be all there was under their tree when Christmas dawned tomorrow. The sky held the promise of more snow. A white Christmas would provide fun and entertainment for the children. As she walked, words floated up from somewhere in her memory, *I know not what the future holds, but I know who holds the future…*

Lord, I don't know what tomorrow will bring, but I know that whatever happens, tomorrow is in Your faithful hands, and I will choose to rest in that knowledge. She began to feel a peace slowly settling over her, and she smiled in gratitude to the Lord, whose birth they were about to celebrate. When she reached her home, she paused, took a deep breath of the brisk Christmas Eve air, and opened the front door.

Stepping into the dim light of the front hall, Mary heard the excited voices of her children. She hung up her coat and scarf and proceeded toward the voices and the warm, inviting kitchen. Thirteen-year-old Caitlyn, ten-year-old Austin, and seven-year-old Savannah looked up.

"Mom!" shouted Savannah. Then they all began to speak at once, stumbling over their words in the excitement of something yet unclear to Mary.

"Stop." She laughed as she held up her hands motioning for them to all stop talking. "One at a time! Caitlyn, why don't you start, okay? What are you so excited about?"

Cailtyn, short for her age with an athletic build and a love of anything social, began, "Well, you know how last week in Sunday School we learned about the true meaning of Christmas? We learned how um, God loved us so much He gave us His Son. And we learned that Christmas is, like, no different than any other holiday if we don't see God's gift for what it is. Jesus is, like, the way to heaven! Mom, I'm so glad to know that Daddy loved Jesus and will be in heaven when we get there. It makes me happy when I think that because I asked Jesus into my heart, I will get to see Dad again."

"Caitlyn, you aren't the only one who will get to see him again!"

"Savannah and me asked Jesus in our hearts, too!" said Austin.

"And Mommy, too!" added Savannah.

Mary smiled, knowing they had strayed from the subject at hand, but she was pleased to see that while the children's knowledge of the Lord was limited to what they could understand at their ages; each one seemed to be consistently growing in that understanding. She was also glad they had the assurance that their daddy was with the Lord and they would someday see him again. That didn't keep any of them from missing him terribly and wishing he were still here. And it didn't answer the questions, "Why them? Why did their daddy have to be killed in a war? Why does it still hurt so much? Why, why, why…" But for now, this assurance helped them live with the questions that would only be answered when they met Jesus face to face.

"Mommy! You aren't listening!" Savannah's high-pitched voice brought Mary out of her thoughts and reminded her that she had yet to hear what was making them so exited.

"Yeah, Mom," added Austin. "My Sunday school teacher said everybody was lost because we didn't have a Savior before Jesus was born. So God gave us what we needed most—Jesus."

"And my teacher said the best thing we can do at Christmas is give something to somebody who has less than we have. It is only by giving something away that we get the bestest thing of all—Jesus!" added Savannah.

"Savannah, we don't have to do anything but ask him into our hearts. We're not saved by works but by faith, remember?" asked Caitlyn.

"Well, it was something like that. She did say we should look for somebody who has less than we have and give them something," said Savannah.

"My teacher said by giving to others, we are sort of remembering what God did for us," said Austin.

"Yeah, that's it!" Savannah said, nodding.

"Anyway, today at school, our teacher told us about a homeless shelter where people who wouldn't, like, have a Christmas dinner, can go and have one. She said serving them Christmas Eve dinner would be like, giving to those who have less than we do. And some people even bring stuff like coats and hats to give to the homeless people. Before you got home, I talked to Colten and Matti, and they said if its okay with you, Uncle James and Aunt Linda will drive all of us to the shelter so we can help serve the homeless tonight for Christmas Eve!"

"Austin, Savannah, and I talked, and we thought that, um, if it is all right with you, we could, like, do that instead of having presents tomorrow. We know we don't have much money, and this is something we can give, and it won't cost anything. Can we, Mommy? Can we go? We have to call Uncle James and Aunt Linda right now so we can get there early!"

The tears Mary had been fighting for the last hour suddenly spilled over and poured down her cheeks. She was overwhelmed with the faithfulness of God and love for her children.

"What's wrong, Momma?" asked Austin.

"Don't cry, Mommy. We don't have to go if you don't want to," said Savannah.

"I'm not crying because I'm sad. I'm crying because you make me so proud and so happy. Of course we can go.

Caitlyn, you can call Uncle James and let him know we'll be ready as soon as they can get here."

Suddenly, she wasn't tired anymore. The children raced through the house, gathering up gloves, hats, and scarves to give to the homeless. A few coats they had outgrown were added for children who might need them. Finally, Mary walked to the hall closet and took out a man's heavy overcoat. She hugged the coat to herself and closed her eyes. She could still smell his cologne, and it brought with it a wave of longing for his arms around her. Suddenly, she realized that the room had grown quiet, and, opening her eyes, she saw the three children watching her.

"Momma, I feel funny giving Daddy's coat away. It feels like we're giving him away," whispered Caitlyn with a quiver in her voice.

"What would Daddy want us to do?" asked Savannah.

"I think we should vote." Austin took his self-appointed position as "man of the family" seriously. In fact, Mary had had more than one discussion with him about the importance of him being a boy and not rushing into being a man. She had tried to help him understand that Jesus was her partner as head of the family and would not let them down. So she smiled at him, and said, "What if we pray and ask Jesus what we should do?"

They all nodded in agreement, and Mary prayed, "Dear Lord Jesus, you know how much we loved and still love Andrew. Would you please help us decide what to do about his coat? We do not want to lose our connection with him, but we don't want to hang on to something you want us to release."

She paused briefly, and before she could continue, Austin said, "Give it away!" "I think so too, Mom," Caitlyn agreed. "Yeah, Mommy. It's really cold outside, and we don't want nobody dying of *frozation* when they could be warm in Daddy's coat!" Savannah added.

Hiding her amusement at Savannah's gift for inventing words, Mary nodded in agreement and continued, "Lord, it seems You have made Your will clear. Now, I ask that You will help us listen to Your voice so we know just the right person to give this coat to. Thank You for Your direction and Your provision. In Your precious name we pray, Amen."

Again, Austin asserted his masculine opinion. "How 'bout let's agree that nobody gives the coat away until he or she knows that it is to the person Jesus wants?"

"What if everyone thinks a different person?" asked Savannah.

Mary could see trouble brewing, so she said, "Children, I think you all know Jesus well enough to know He would never want you to quarrel over a gift of any kind. So I am going to trust you to agree among yourselves about who should receive this coat. I know this is a very special gift from you. We will leave this coat in the box, and when one of you thinks you know who is supposed to get it, discuss it with the each other and, might I add, ask Jesus if it is the right person. Then, when you agree, you go ahead and give the coat away. You don't have to ask me. I trust you and your relationship with your daddy and with Jesus."

They all nodded solemnly as if they had just received an all-important—even holy—commission. And, in a way, they had. Mary thought of the offering of the widow's mite, the story in the Bible about a widow who gave a tiny offering in the temple. Jesus praised her to his disciples, telling them that all the others had given out of their abundance, but this woman had given everything she had. She gave out of her need. Mary's children were willing to give one of the last physical reminders of their dad to someone who had a need. It was not exactly the same thing, but it was in the same spirit, to be sure.

As she folded the coat to put it in the box, her eye caught a glimpse of gold on the collar. She removed a small pin and handed it to Savannah. "Here, honey, I think it would be okay for you to keep this. It won't make the coat warmer, and I know it is special to you since you gave it to Daddy."

Savannah reached out her hand, closing it tenderly around the small pin. As she did, Mary was struck with how small her hand was. "Lord," she said to herself, "she has had to grow up too fast! She is my baby and has already suffered too much loss in her young life."

Mary. The words were not audible, but she heard them clearly in the quiet of her heart. *Don't you know I count the very hairs on her head? I will care for her, and she will grow to minister to others out of her own loss. Trust Me with her, and trust Me with yourself.*

Quietly, she placed the coat in the box and closed the lid. As she did, they heard a horn honking in the driveway.

"Uncle James is here!" The children were dancing with excitement.

Somehow, they managed to get everything and everybody tucked into the van, and they were on their way. Mary said a silent prayer of gratitude for her brother and his wife and for the fact that they had a van big enough to hold all of them. When Andrew was killed and she became the only breadwinner, she had decided to sell the family car. Not only could she not afford the payments, she couldn't afford the upkeep and insurance. The children caught the bus to school, and she was able to ride the city bus to work and to shop. Even though she missed the convenience of having a car, she couldn't justify the added expense. Maybe someday she could have a car again, but it was a small sacrifice compared to the blessings she held dear. Her faith, her children, and her family were the things she truly cherished. They were blessings that money could not buy and for which she thanked the Lord every day.

Four

By the time they reached the homeless shelter, the children's excitement had reached a fever pitch. They sang Christmas carols all the way, and when they arrived, the laughter and fun spilled out as they unloaded themselves and their offerings.

Linda, whose quiet, calming manner made it easy to underestimate her ability to turn chaos into calm, directed everyone to the right entrance. She was familiar with the facility since she had been here before as a volunteer.

"Linda! I'm so glad to see you again! I see you came with Santa's helpers in tow!" A stately woman started toward them from across the crowded room. Her flawless skin was the color of creamy caramel, and her thick, dark hair was pulled back into a bun at the nape of her neck. Tall and graceful, she seemed to float across the room.

"Ophelia, I see you are still manning the troops. Family, I would like you to meet Ophelia. The only thing greater than her ability to organize, is her huge love for mankind. Ophelia, you've met my husband, James, and our children, Matti and Colten. I'd like you to meet James's sister, Mary, and her children Caitlyn, Austin, and Savannah."

"Mary, the pleasure is all mine." She took Mary's outstretched hand in both of hers. "And how, Mister James, did a poor excuse like yourself fall in with such a handsome group of relatives?"

"Just lucky, I guess." James grinned.

"Luck has nothing to do with it," retorted Ophelia. "God has blessed you, my friend. His grace is no respecter of persons for sure." She chuckled.

"Mommy," Savannah tugged on Mary's sleeve and whispered in a stage whisper. "She's so pretty!"

"Child. I think I need a dose of you every day! Can I put you in my pocket and keep you?" Ophelia laughed.

Savannah squirmed in embarrassment but was nevertheless pleased with the woman's acknowledgement.

"Ophelia!" came a call from across the room.

She looked and held up her finger in a "give me one minute" gesture.

"Linda, you know the drill. If you and Mary can help me serve, and James can haul things back and forth from the kitchen, that would be great. And the children can help keep the tables picked up and fill in where needed. Please don't forget to speak to our guests. They get so little respect from the world. I think they forget they have worth. And, speaking of respect, if you meet someone who doesn't want to talk, respect that too, just like you would with each other. Now let's get this show on the road, and don't forget to enjoy yourselves! It's Christmas Eve!"

With that, she turned and moved back across the room. Linda showed the group where they could put their own coats and the things they brought to give away. The hollow sound of feet shuffling on old, wood floors filled the dining hall, and the smell of turkey and dressing gave the old building a festive, almost homey atmosphere. As Mary, Linda, and James moved toward the serving line, the children scampered toward the tables and the evening's guests.

The next two hours seemed to melt away as Mary and Linda helped Ophelia. They served, smiled, and talked to the guests. While they worked, they each kept one eye on the children, as mothers do.

Colten, tall for his thirteen years, as well as being a handsome boy, had a gift for conversing with folks of all ages. An honor student, he was just beginning to discover his athletic talents, beginning his second year of wrestling and completing his first year of football. Colten had always been a very kind child and had every indication of being the same as a teenager. He was often quiet and reflective, and Mary had been struck with the intelligence of the questions he asked about faith and the Bible. Right now, he was deep in conversation with a couple of the guests.

As she watched, Colten scooted his chair closer to the two men. He nodded his head in response to what was being said. Then he leaned in as if the three of them were part of a conspiratorial secret, and said something behind his hand. The three exploded in laughter and gave each other a high five. Another man approached the three, and as introductions were made, Colten rose and gave his chair to the newcomer, retrieving another for himself.

Mary smiled with pride for her nephew, and looked across the room at Matti. Fourteen-year-old Matti was rarely seen without a sketchpad, and that night was no exception. As she talked with various guests, her pencil moved nonstop on the pad in front of her. Mary noticed several of the departing guests holding a folded-up memento of their evening.

That's our Matti, thought Mary, *so giving and generous.* Matti was also an honor student and was already making her plans for college. She was a good example for Caitlyn, and Mary was grateful her children had such wonderful cousins.

Caitlyn was in the thick of activity, as usual. She had managed to round up a group of small children and was entertaining them with stories and games. *Never a dull moment with Caitlyn!* thought Mary with a smile. Caitlyn was a good student, but she had to make herself attend to her studies. For her, school had always been about the social interaction. Softball was her sport of choice, and it suited her short, compact body well. But even that was more about the team than about the sport.

Oh, Andrew! How I wish you were here! The children need a father's love, example, and protection! Caitlyn is at such a tender, impressionable point in her young life. Will I be able to be what she needs?

Again, the Lord spoke to her heart in His still, soft way, *Mary, remember, I am the father of the fatherless. I will walk beside you and beside them. There is nothing this life can hand them that I can't guide them through. Remember, my ways are not your ways. Trust me.*

"Oh, Lord, I *do* trust You, and I believe You. Please help me in my weakness and my doubt," Mary whispered to herself. She was reminded of something her pastor had said just last Sunday. *Faith is not the absence of doubt, but the presence of belief in the midst of doubt.* She smiled as she remembered and thanked the Lord once again for His faithfulness to her and the children.

Looking over the crowded room, she spotted her son. Austin possessed a tenacity that could be a challenge when his views opposed hers but, when properly channeled, was a gift. Right now he was jostling with a small group of boys about his age. The body language for little boys is universal, thought Mary with a smile. She watched as Austin began to search through his pockets and pulled out four or five matchbox cars. The boys retreated to the back of the hall, and he gave each of them a car. Then they proceeded to engage in a spirited and slightly raucous racecar competition. Mary looked at Ophelia and raised her eyebrows in question.

"Don't give it a worry. This is probably the first time those boys have had this much fun in a long time. Let them be. Heaven knows life will get serious again all too soon. Besides, look at that boy of yours, he looks like the cat that swallowed the canary. No way I'm going to deprive him the joy of giving."

Scanning the room, Mary noticed that Savannah was sitting with an older man who had distanced himself from the others by taking a small table to the side. His hair was long and hung in unwashed strings around his face. He wore a long dirty trench coat over nearly threadbare clothes. Even from this distance, Mary could see the grime on his hands and under his nails. None of that seemed to concern Savannah, however. Mary noted that almost from the moment he sat down, Savannah had been sitting with him. During a lull in the serving line, Mary leaned over to Ophelia and asked about him. "What can you tell me about that man?"

"Oh, that is Max, and I have never seen him talk to anyone before. He always stays to himself and leaves immediately after he eats. I have tried to talk to him on several occasions, and he merely shrugs or grunts. From what I can gather from others, he used to be a very wealthy man. About five years ago on Christmas Eve, a drunk driver hit the car Max was driving. His wife and small daughter were killed instantly; he alone survived the crash. Totally devastated, he simply walked away and never returned. I hear that his niece has been managing his estate in hopes that he would someday return."

"That's very sad," responded Mary. "I will certainly be praying for him. I know the pain of loss all too well. I am still going to keep my eye on them, however. Savannah may remind him of his own daughter, but she is very innocent; I just want to keep her safe."

"I don't blame you, especially with the stories we hear on the news these days. While I really don't think you have anything to fear from Max, I confess that I have been keeping my eye on them, too. My interest, however, is equal parts caution and curiosity.

"Well, here comes another wave of folks. I guess our break is over! This will probably be the last group of the night."

• ● ●

The dining hall was almost empty, and the kitchen crew was in full cleanup mode. "They sure don't stay long, do they?" observed Mary to Ophelia.

"Most of them will be headed for the warming shelters for the night," Ophelia responded. "You should have seen it before the city opened the warming shelters for them. Most would just take their food with them so they could stake a claim someplace where they could at least be out of the wind."

Mary noticed that Max and Savannah were still chatting at his table. "Before tonight, I guess I thought most homeless people were here because they had made bad choices, were not motivated, or were on drugs. But after hearing Max's story, I realize there are probably as many reasons for being homeless as there are homeless people."

"You are *so* right. Yes, there are some who are on the streets because it is simply the lifestyle they have chosen. But even they have a story. Some started out as runaways from abusive homes. Some got hooked on drugs or alcohol, and this is the end result of those choices. Some lost jobs and homes because of the state of our economy. And some, like Max, endured some tragedy from which they simply have not been able to recover. Whatever the reason, we need to remember that God loves each one of them the same way He loves us. Jesus died for them, and the truth is, without Him, we are all hopelessly without a hope or a home."

"I have a confession to make," Mary continued. "Earlier tonight, I was feeling pretty sorry for myself. I think I have some repenting to do. I was so wrapped up in my own problems that I failed to see how blessed I really am. I have a job. I have a home. I have three beautiful children and a loving family. And, most importantly, I have a loving heavenly Father and Savior to walk with me through the tough times."

Ophelia placed her hand on Mary's shoulder. "In the name of Jesus, I speak forgiveness to you. From what I hear, you have had more than your share of challenges this year. Don't be too hard on yourself. Just accept God's lesson and go on. The Word instructs us to confess our faults to one another. This is not so our faults can be used as a form of flagellation—quite the opposite. By confessing, the hidden things lose their hold on us, and the enemy can no longer use them against us. You are an amazing young woman, and the love of Christ shines in and through you. Just continue to put your trust in Him, and I am confident that He will be faithful to take care of you and your children. If you ever need someone to pray with or vent to, please do not hesitate to call me. Sometimes a person needs someone who is not as close to the situation as family."

Again, Mary's eyes stung with unshed tears. "Thank you. I feel like we have been friends for years. I didn't realize how much I missed being able to just be real with someone. Andrew was the one I could always vent with and who kept me grounded. Without him, I feel like I have been floating without an anchor. I know the Lord is my strength, and I couldn't have made it through the past year without him. But as the saying goes, sometimes I need someone with skin on!"

Ophelia's deep, throaty chuckle warmed Mary's heart. "Girl, you're talk'n to the choir there! And speaking of someone with skin on, look at that little girl of yours with Max. I have never seen him respond to anyone like that before. Even if Max had responded to folks, most would have been turned away by his filth and smell and would have kept their distance, anyway. But that child of yours doesn't seem to even notice."

Linda walked up then and said, "James is out warming up the van. I think it's time to get these guys home."

Mary had been so focused on her conversation with Ophelia that she hadn't noticed that the hall was quiet, and her family had gathered at the door with coats in hand. That is, all except Savannah, who was still talking to Max.

"Savannah!" called Mary. "We need to be going now. Say good-bye to your friend and come get your coat."

"Okay, Mommy," responded Savannah, and she jumped up and started across the room. Suddenly, she stopped and ran back to Max. Reaching up to brush back his dirty hair, she stood on tiptoe and whispered something in his ear. In response, he slowly brought his arms up and tenderly, as if he were afraid she would break, he hugged the little girl. Savannah wrapped her arms around his shoulders and returned the hug. She then turned and skipped across the room to join her family.

Watching, Mary was sure she saw tears in the man's eyes. Slowly he stood; head down and without saying a word, he walked to the door and disappeared into the night.

Five

The ride home was quiet. Mary was thankful that Ophelia had insisted on feeding the family before they began serving others. In the excitement of the moment, nobody had thought about their own dinner before they left home. The children nodded off in their seats, and the adults were either equally as tired or deep in thought. Linda broke the silence. "It sure makes you think about what we take for granted, doesn't it?"

"Yes it does. In fact, I said pretty much the same thing to Ophelia just before we left," said Mary. She looked at the children and felt her heart swell with love for her family. "I am so thankful for all of you and for God's provision for us."

"I feel the same way. I never dreamed that when I married James, I would inherit the family I never had. I wish your mom and dad could have made the trip to be with us,"

"So do I," said James, "but even though it is only a hundred miles, the weather and roads can be dangerous and unpredictable this time of year. I would rather know they are safe. We can have a family gathering when the roads clear up. If we get the snow they predict tonight, the short distance between your house and ours is about as far as I want to be traveling myself,"

"Speaking of between your house and ours, James and I were talking, and instead of us bringing you to our house tomorrow, how about if we pack up our dinner fix'ns and bring them to your house in the morning? That would reduce the traveling to one trip instead of two," asked Linda.

"I'm so sorry you have to always be the ones to drive. As soon as I can, I will get us a car, but I just can't justify the debt right now."

"Really, we don't mind, I just thought it would be easier for all of us. Savannah is so pooped. She can get up and just stay in her PJs for a while, and you and I can get the bird in the oven. James can keep one eye on the kids while he keeps the other one on the game," said Linda.

"Actually, that sounds great. I have to admit that I would love to lounge in my pajamas for a little bit, myself!" answered Mary.

"That settles it, then. It won't be at the crack of dawn. We'll let these two take their time in the morning too, and they can decide what they want to bring with them for entertainment. I'm so glad they are not expecting all the latest gadgets and games as some kids do these days. If they were, they would be sorely disappointed with their Christmas. James and I decided, and the children agreed, to keep our Christmas giving to simple gestures of our love for one another and for our Savior. We even encouraged that the gifts be handmade, but that isn't mandatory."

Mary suspected that one of the factors her brother's family had taken into consideration was her own financial situation. If everyone kept it simple, she would not feel so badly about not having the means to do much for her family. How she loved them for their thoughtfulness. Her own simple, handmade gifts would be the status quo for the entire family. She had a feeling that it was going to make for a very special day for all of them. They would focus on their love for each other, their family tradition, and on the gift of their Savior, given so many years ago.

Savannah was sound asleep when they reached Mary's house. Austin was seriously close, and even Caitlyn, Colten, and Matti were beginning to succumb to the cozy warmth of the van.

James got out and took Savannah in his arms. "Come here, you little munchkin. Let your uncle carry you in. Besides, I love having the excuse to hug on you a little."

Mary released Austin from his seat belt and half carried, half guided him to the house while Caitlyn said sleepy good-byes to her cousins. "See you tomorrow. Merry Christmas! Let's play Scrabble tomorrow. I need a chance to get even with you, Colten!"

Mary smiled. "Even when half asleep, the girl is planning a party!"

They followed James and Savannah into the house and up the stairs to the bedrooms. Mary guided Austin into his room and turned to rescue James from his sleeping bundle. Once she got Savannah's coat off, she shucked her shoes and trousers off and tucked her between soft, flannel sheets. She instructed Caitlyn to brush her teeth and get herself to bed while she headed down the stairs.

At the door, Mary hugged her big brother and said, "I love you so much. Thank you for being here for me and for the children. They miss Andrew so much."

"What are big brothers for if not to help …and torment their sisters? Besides, Andrew was my brother, and I miss him too. When I see those children, I see him. I love all of you, and I'm thankful that I can be here for you. I would not have it any other way, and Linda feels the same."

"Speaking of Linda, you better get out there and get her and the children home. She may not be so accommodating if you keep her out there all night!"

"Okay, sis." James gave her another hug. "We'll see you in the morning. You get some sleep and remember how much you are loved."

Mary sniffed back a tear, "Thanks, bro. I love you, too, and Merry Christmas! See you in a frighteningly few hours!"

With that, she pushed him out the door. As she did, she noticed that snow was again falling from the night sky. "Lord, it does look like a white Christmas for us. Please keep them safe on the road and bless them."

Closing and locking the door, she turned and slowly made her way into the living room. After turning on the Christmas lights, she returned to the kitchen to make a cup of herbal tea. She was a bit wound up from the evening and needed some time to relax and reflect.

"Mom?" She turned to see Austin in the doorway. "I miss Dad."

"Would you like to have a cup of hot chocolate with me?" He nodded, and she reached for the Ovaltine. *No caffeine for you, bud,* she thought.

A few minutes later, they sat in front of the Christmas tree, sipping their tea and "hot chocolate."

"Mom, can Daddy see us from heaven?" asked Austin.

"Well now, I don't really know the answer to that," Mary said softly. "I know that the Bible tells us there are no tears in heaven, so I know that Daddy wouldn't see anything that would make him sad. But I also know that in heaven, you see things the way God sees them, so things that might make you sad on earth, may not make you sad if you could see the whole picture the way God does."

"You didn't answer my question," Austin protested.

"My little lawyer in the making." Mary laughed softy. "I guess I would have to say, I simply don't know the answer to your question. There are some things about heaven we won't ever know until we get there ourselves."

That seemed to satisfy him, at least for the time being.

"And now, my little man, you need to go to bed. It is already Christmas morning, and you need to get some sleep. Did you brush your teeth?"

"Yeah, but do I need to do it again since I drank hot chocolate?"

"I think you will be fine. Just brush them when you get up, okay? "

"Mommy, will you pray with me before I go to bed?"

Austin switched between still calling her Mommy and shortening it to the more grownup 'Mom.' It often depended on how vulnerable he was feeling at the moment. Caitlyn most often called her 'Mom,' and Savannah was the opposite; more often than not, she still defaulted to 'Mommy.' As she so often did, Mary thought of all the changes and events that Andrew would never experience.

"Mommy?"

"Yes, Austin, I will pray with you." She took his hand in hers and, closing her eyes, she paused a moment to listen to the Holy Spirit.

"Oh, Father, we thank You so much for showing us tonight how blessed we really are. We thank You for our family and our home. We thank You that even though we miss Andrew so terribly much, You gave him to us for awhile, and we did a lot of living in that time. We thank You for the assurance that someday we will be reunited with him and never have to say good-bye again. Now, I ask You to watch over our home this night and help us to remember why we celebrate tomorrow. Help us to remember the greatest gift ever given to anyone, the gift of Your Son. Please help Austin to sleep well and rest in Your love for him. I ask these things in the precious name of Your gift to us, the name of Jesus. Amen."

"Amen," repeated Austin, followed by a hug for Mary. "Good night, Mommy, and, oh yes! Merry Christmas!"

"Good night, my love. Sweet dreams, and I will see you in the morning."

As Austin padded up the stairs, Mary returned to the kitchen for another cup of tea. She knew she should be going to bed herself but still needed a bit of time to unwind before she would be able to sleep. Usually, she would read before going to sleep, but that night she just wanted to sit quietly and watch the Christmas lights.

While her tea water heated, she retrieved from her bedroom the few packages for her children, which she had hidden there. What she had considered inadequate a few hours before now seemed to be just right. As she arranged the packages under the tree, she noticed four small packages tucked among the branches.

"What do we have here?" she asked herself. Picking them up, she noticed they were addressed, one to each of the children, and one to her. She recognized the handwriting as belonging to James. "He shouldn't have done that," she mused to herself. "Yet it was not unlike him to do so. "Just having him and Linda and the children here tomorrow is enough to make our Christmas complete."

She retrieved her tea, and, cradling the warm mug in her hands, she curled up in Andrew's favorite chair. The room felt so intimate and warm that she felt herself really relaxing for the first time that day. The twinkling lights seemed to mesmerize her, and the familiar ticking sounds of the house calmed her weary mind. She sensed the presence of the Lord, but felt no compulsion to speak. In the quiet, she thought back over the last nine months. What anger she had struggled with the first couple of months after loosing Andrew! People told her it was normal, but it hadn't felt normal. It had felt, like everything else at that time, foreign and intrusive. She remembered times when the children were with her parents, when she had indulged in some real dish shattering episodes of anger. But, even if the anger was understandable and as so many told her, *normal*, it never brought Andrew back. Not only did it not bring him back, but it left her feeling even more vulnerable and adrift.

Slowly however, without even realizing she was doing it, she had begun to focus her attention on what she still had: her children, her home, her family, and her faith. She thought back to the conversation she had with herself before getting out of bed this morning. And for the first time she realized that, although she may indeed be taking baby steps, she actually *was* getting better!

Talk about not seeing the forest for the trees, she thought. I have been so enmeshed in just getting through each day, that I have not noticed that I am beginning to feel some sense of purpose again. She remembered a scripture verse, she thought it was from the Psalms that said, "A wounded reed He will not break." She had certainly been wounded, severely wounded, but He had not allowed her to be broken.

Mary thought of yet another scripture passage, this time she was sure it was from the book of Deuteronomy. God, speaking to the Israelites said, "I have set before you life and death...therefore choose life that both you and your descendants may live."

In the quiet of the moment, as she rested in His presence she whispered, "Thank you Lord Jesus. I know I will continue to miss Andrew, and I know the future will not be easy, but right now, for me and for my children, I choose life…"

Six

"Mommy! Wake up! It's Christmas!" Savannah's excited call reached her through a thick fog of sleep. She felt herself being shaken and slowly opened one eye. Three sets of eyes stared back at her.

"Why are you sleeping in Daddy's chair?" asked Savannah.

"Are you all right, Mom?" added Cailtyn, looking worried.

"Mom, you're still wearing your yesterday clothes," said Austin.

Mary sat up and stretched. Looking at the clock, she exclaimed, "I guess I fell asleep last night and slept all the way through!" Actually, she had fallen into a very sound sleep, something she rarely did since they lost Andrew, and she felt more rested than she could remember feeling in a very long time. Once she was moving, however, she felt her muscles rebelling from the curled up position in which she had slept.

"Tell you what, can you give Mommy a few minutes to take a hot shower and change into something comfortable before we get things started?"

"I'll make you some coffee," said Caitlyn.

"I'll turn on the Christmas music," added Austin.

"What can I do?" asked Savannah.

"How about you run up and brush your teeth? You were sound asleep when Uncle James carried you to bed last night, so you didn't get them brushed then," said Mary.

"Uncle James! Then who took my jeans off and put me to bed?"

"Not to worry, baby girl. Uncle James just carried you into the bedroom for me. I put you to bed. Now, let's go upstairs and get ready while your brother and sister take care of things down here."

"Okie-dokie," she chirped and bounded ahead of Mary up the stairs.

Twenty minutes later, they were all sitting in the living room, and Mary, wearing jeans and a sweatshirt, was sipping a cup of coffee. "Caitlyn, good job on the coffee! Now can you hand me my Bible so we can read the Christmas story?"

She opened her Bible to that familiar passage in the second chapter of Luke. They had always started their Christmas morning by reading this passage and having a discussion about the real meaning of Christmas. As she began to read, she could almost feel Andrew's smile. *He would be pleased to know that we are continuing our family tradition*, she thought.

"And it came to pass in those days that a decree went out from Caesar Augustus…"

•   •   •

 When she finished reading, they remained quiet. As usual, Savannah was the first to speak.

"Mommy, what does it mean that Mary was 'great with child'?"

"It means that she was very close to giving birth. It probably means that her tummy was very big. 'Great' sometimes means 'big,'" answered Mary.

Savannah seemed to give this some thought, then she asked, "Mommy, were you 'great' with me?"

Mary laughed. "Yes, Savannah. I was very 'great' with you!"

"You have the same name as Jesus's mommy!" continued Savannah.

"Yes, I do. A lot of people have the same name as someone else. The name Mary is a very common name."

"There is a boy in my class at school named Johnny, and he was mean to my friend, and when I hear that name, I think of him, so I don't like nobody named Johnny," Savannah stated soundly.

"Savannah, that isn't fair. Just 'cause somebody has the same name as somebody else doesn't mean they are *like* that person!" said Austin.

"Well, when I hear that name, I think of the mean person, so it *seems* like it is the same thing," she responded.

"It's just not cool to judge people from what it seems like at first. Like, remember when I first met Holly? I didn't think I was going to like her 'cause I thought she was stuck up. But when I, like, got to know her, I learned that she was just really shy, and now she's my BFF!" said Caitlyn.

"How did my little girl get so wise?" asked Mary. "You are growing up to be a beautiful young woman inside and out, and I am so proud of you. And speaking of not judging, I want you all to know I was very proud of you last night. You conducted yourselves like young ladies and gentleman, and I believe you made Christmas a little brighter for some people."

"By the way," she continued, "I noticed we didn't bring Daddy's coat home. I assume you all agreed on who received it?"

The children looked at each other and smiled. They squirmed in anticipation. "You will never guess who we gave it to," said Austin. The girls giggled and clapped their hands together. "We gave it to…"

"A *lady*!" shouted Savannah, unable to keep still any longer.

"A lady?" asked Mary.

"Yeah, a lady. We all saw her just as she was leaving. She was carrying one of Matti's pictures, and she didn't have a coat on—just a little sweater," said Austin.

"Yeah, Mommy. She didn't even have *none* coat! We were afraid she would get *frozation*!" Savannah added.

"She didn't have *any* coat, and we didn't want her to freeze, so we all agreed that she should have Daddy's coat," Austin said.

"Momma, remember how Daddy told us that the reason he went to war was to protect us? Well, we thought it would be kinda cool to think that Daddy was still protecting, even though he can't be here anymore. His last gift was to protect somebody from the cold," Caitlyn said.

"Oh, Lord Jesus," whispered Mary, "how you have blessed me with these children. Please let me remember this moment the next time I am frustrated or impatient with them!"

She hugged each one to herself and wished she could put this moment in a capsule so she could re-live it the next time she was feeling sorry for herself.

"Mommy! We made you something!" Austin exclaimed as if he had just remembered.

"Yes, we did!" added Cailtyn as she rose and went over to the tree. She retrieved a flat package that was about twelve inches, square, and wrapped with lots of tape.

Making a show of slowly, laboriously unwrapping the package, Mary pulled back the paper and looked inside.

A piece of cardboard had been covered with fabric. Over the fabric, strips of ribbon had been arranged in a criss-cross pattern. Tucked into the grid created by the ribbons were pictures of their family. Some were pictures of just the children, some were of her and the children, and in the center was a snapshot taken of all five of them, Andrew in uniform, just before he left for the last time.

"Oh my! This is wonderful. I love it!" she said in surprise.

"We learned how to do it in Sunday school, and I showed Austin and Savannah." "Then we all decided it would be a good present for you. I hope its okay that we used some of your fabric and ribbons," said Caitlyn.

"It's more than okay. It is smart, innovative, and resourceful. Besides, I absolutely love it. Thank you all so much."

"What's inno, inno…" Savannah stumbled.

"'Innovative. It means to make something new out of what you already have. It takes imagination and creativity, and it is something that a lot of people have forgotten how to do."

"Now, if you look closely under the tree, I think you will find some things under there with your names on them."

They quickly retrieved the small packages Mary had placed there the night before, and they made short work of tearing the paper off to reveal their treasures. Mary had managed to purchase each child a new pair of gloves. To those, she had added scarves and hats she crocheted in the evenings after the children were in bed.

The children laughed when they saw what was in their packages. "Thank you, Mommy! We gave all ours away last night!" said Savannah.

"These will make my coat look just like new. I love the colors, Momma. Thank you," said Caitlyn.

Austin gave Mary a big hug. "Thank you, Mom. These will keep my ears warm, for sure. Now I can play outside with Matti and Colten today and not freeze!"

Mary got up and went to the tree. Carefully she retrieved the mysterious packages her brother had somehow placed among the branches without her knowledge. As she did, she noticed an envelope that had escaped her attention the previous evening. It said, also in James's handwriting, "Open First." "Hmmm, she said. What is he up to?"

She slowly sat back down as the children watched in puzzlement. "Uncle James left these things in our tree last night. Let's have a look." She placed the small, wrapped boxes in her lap and opened the envelope. When she unfolded the stationary, her breath caught, and tears immediately stung the backs of her eyes.

She would recognize Andrew's bold scrawl anywhere. "It's from Daddy!" she exclaimed. "But how..."

"Read it, Mommy!" The children crowded around her, all speaking at once.

Mary cleared her throat and read:

• • •

My Dear Family,

If you are reading this, it means that it is Christmas. It also means it will be your first Christmas knowing I won't be coming home. First, let me say I am sorry. I had such dreams of us all growing together and watching you become adults. I thought I would live to see my grandchildren. But God had other plans for me—and for you.

Although I don't understand, by the time you read this, I will. The most important thing to know is that I trust God. I trust that He loves you even more than I do, which, my dear family, is more than you could even imagine. I trust that He will watch over you all and will guide you into the life He has for you.

Please, dear ones, talk to Him about your feelings. Be honest with Him, and let Him help you. He understands your pain, your grief, and, yes, even your anger. He has very broad shoulders and can handle anything you tell Him.

Savannah, do you remember when you came home from Sunday school and told me about the bumblebee? I want you all to remember the lesson of the bumblebee.

The bumblebee is a mystery. Because of how it is built, a bumblebee should not be able to fly. Its body is the wrong size and shape, and its wings are too small. But we all know that bumblebees *do* fly. How do they do it? Well, now that is the mystery of the bumblebee. But what seems impossible to man, is possible with God.

Sometimes life is like that. We don't understand things, and we try to figure it out with our minds. But there are things we will never understand with our minds. That's when we have to trust God. What we don't understand, He does. What we think is impossible, God makes possible.

Remember what the apostle Paul said: "I can do all things through Christ who gives me strength." If you think of Paul as God's bumblebee, you will remember that you too can be God's bumblebee. You can do what others tell you is impossible. If you learn to dream with God, you will become what He wants you to become. And remember, I love you all more than words could ever express.

Now, I have something for each one of you, to help you remember what I have said. I gave these things, along with this letter, to Uncle James before I left. I knew there was a possibility that I wouldn't be returning. So I told him if that happened to make sure you received these things, along with this letter on your first Christmas without me.

Remember, the day will come when there will be no more good-byes. Until then, my treasures, stay faithful to God and to each other.

Love forever,
Daddy

• • •

The room was silent. None of them wanted to break the spell of hearing Andrew's words again. It was beyond anything they had imagined would happen all these months after he was taken from them.

Finally, Mary reached into her lap for the small packages there. One at a time, she handed each child the last gift they would receive from their daddy.

Cailtyn opened the small card attached to the outside of her box.

• • •

My darling firstborn,

I will never forget the first time I saw your beautiful little face. I couldn't believe how lucky I was! Mom says you spent the first two years of your life in my pocket. And now you are getting so grown up. Always remember who you are. You are a child of God. Nothing life can hand you will change that truth. As you grow up, you will be faced with many challenges. Remember, if God says it is possible, nothing man says can change it. Be true to yourself and to God. Listen to your mother, even when you don't want to, or when she sounds old fashioned and out of touch. She is a wise woman and loves you beyond words. Know, my sweet girl, how proud I am of you and how very, very much I love you. Merry Christmas, Pumpkin.

    Love,
    Dad

• • •

Caitlyn brushed away tears and slowly opened the small box that had come with the note. In it, she found two, tiny, gold bumblebees. They were earrings for pierced ears.

"How did Daddy know I wanted to get my ears pierced?" she exclaimed. Oh, Momma, they are so pretty. Now I will always remember the story of the bumblebee!

Next, Savannah opened the small envelope attached to her package. She asked Mary to read the note for her.

• • •

Dear Savannah,

    By now, you know that I remember our talk about the bumble bee. You, my dear daughter, have a gift for grasping the things of God. Don't lose that curiosity and wonder for learning about Him. He will continue to teach you all of your days if you will listen. When you remember the bumblebee, remember that you too can fly. You can fly in your spirit with God to discover His plans for you. I love you, baby girl, to the moon and back and beyond! Someday, we will explore the beyond together. Until then, remember that you are never alone. God is always with you. Jesus is always holding your hand, and my love and prayers for you will continue to go before the throne of God for all of your days. Merry Christmas, my beautiful baby girl.

Love,
Daddy

• • •

Savannah opened her small gift and exclaimed, "It's a bumblebee necklace! Oh, Mommy, it is so pretty! Now I have a bumblebee, too!"

"But Savannah, what about—" began Caitlyn. But she was interrupted by her brother.

Anxious to see what was in his package, Austin exclaimed, "My turn!" and he opened his own envelope.

• • •

Dear Austin,

You are my boy. How did I get so blessed to have such a fine boy as you for my son? You are smart and faithful, and I know you will want to be the man of the family once I am gone. Son, I want you to finish being a boy before you become a man. God will take care of our family, and Jesus will partner with your mom to make sure she is all right. As you grow, no doubt you will take on more responsibility. But trust your mom to know how much and how soon, okay? I know it may look to you like things aren't being done the right way. When that happens, I want you to remember the bumblebee. Even though you don't understand something, it doesn't always mean it isn't right. It's okay to express your opinion, but always respect your mother as having the final word. By trusting and honoring her, you are honoring me, and you are placing your trust in God. I am so very proud of you, son. I know God has big plans for you. Listen for His voice, and watch for His direction, and you will accomplish much for Him in this world. Always know how proud I am to be your Dad. Merry Christmas, my son.

Love,
Dad

• • •

As Austin slowly unwrapped his package, Mary could see tears in his eyes. Out of the tissue paper, Austin lifted a key ring. The fob was leather and shaped like a bumblebee. Truly a work of art, the leather was carved in painstaking detail of a bumblebee in flight. "Wow!" exclaimed Austin. "I was afraid I was going to get jewelry, too, and I didn't know what I would do with it. But this is awesome! I can keep my house key on it so I won't lose it. I will keep it with me always to remember Daddy and remember the lesson of the bumblebee."

"Now you, mommy! Now you!" Savannah said, clapping her hands.

Mary, hands trembling with emotion, opened the envelope addressed to her.

• • •

My dearest Mary,

I can only imagine how hard these past months have been for you. I am so sorry you have to go through this without me. Please know it is not what I ever wanted, but I guess you know that already. I don't know what God's plans are for you now, but I do know that you are safe in His care. Even though I know you won't want to, please accept the help James and Linda will offer. It won't be forever, just until you find your wings again. And you will find them again, my love. You may not think so, but just like the bumblebee shouldn't be able to fly—it flies. God will show you how to fly again. Trust Him. Remember that all things are possible to him who believes. Believe in God and His mighty faithfulness. Speaking of flying again, when the time is right, you will love again. Don't expect it to be like ours; it won't be. But that doesn't mean it will not be as blessed or fulfilling. Love is as varied and unique as the people it envelops. When it happens, embrace it completely as you did ours. Never feel like you are being unfaithful to what we had. Life goes on; so must you. I give you my blessing in advance and assure you that it is what I want for you. Fly, my love. Soar with God on wings as eagles and never doubt His ability to accomplish in and through you what seems impossible.

You were the love of my life. Always remember that.

—Andrew

* * *

Mary could barely see through her tears as she opened the tiny box in front of her. She parted the tissue and removed a tiny charm. It was, of course, a bumblebee. One of the first gifts she had ever received from Andrew was a gold charm bracelet. It now contained many charms, mementos of their life together. She held the tiny charm close to her heart and thought to herself, *Oh, Andrew, I don't want to fly again! I feel as if my wings have been forever clipped. But I promise I will place my hand in the hand of Jesus and walk with Him one day at a time. I will do that for you, my darling. For you.*

"Group hug!" announced Caitlyn.

As they all came together in a long, tearful hug, it was as if a sweet aroma swept through and around them. It was the closure they had all been craving since Andrew's death. It hadn't happened at the memorial service. It hadn't happened at the gravesite. It hadn't happened as they sorted through Andrew's belongings, deciding what to keep and what to give away. It hadn't even happened when they gave away his overcoat. But slowly, as they stood together with Andrew's own words settling over them, they released the worst of the anguish. It wasn't gone entirely, but the pain no longer controlled them. It no longer felt as if it would consume their every thought and action. Now the memories seemed to take on a bittersweet quality that was bearable, even embraceable.

"Lord Jesus," Mary began quietly, "thank You for giving each of us one last gift from Andrew. At last we can begin to rebuild our lives with you. Help us to do so wisely and to honor all that You are and all that Andrew stood for. And now, Lord, please bless the rest of our day—this, the first Christmas of the rest of our lives. We give it to You, and we give our lives to You anew. Help us to remember the bumblebee and the lessons we can learn from this tiny insect that You created. In Your precious name we ask these things. Amen."

"And now, my little bumblebees, let's pick up the wrappings and get ready for Uncle James and Aunt Linda. They will be here before we know it. I need to get some things started in the kitchen for dinner."

As if on cue, the doorbell rang, and the children stampeded to open the door. Snow blew in along with Matti, Linda, Colten, and James, each carrying a covered dish or bag of food. "Merry Christmas!" Everyone was talking at once, and hugs were exchanged all around.

"Aunt Linda!" Savannah's squeaky voice carried above the din. "Mommy said I'm invasive!" she beamed.

Linda raised an eyebrow at Mary. "And that's a *good* thing?"

"Innovative." Mary laughed. "The children made me a Christmas gift, and I told them they were innovative."

"Yeah!" said Savannah proudly.

"Well, my darling, I would say you certainly are innovative and much more!" Linda hugged Savannah. "Now, Aunt Linda needs to get this turkey in the oven. It's all ready to go in. We just need to turn the oven on."

James closed the door as he carried the last of the dinner supplies in from the van. As he did, he caught Mary's eye. "Thank you," she mouthed.

He crossed the room and enveloped her in a big hug. "You're welcome, sis. I wish I could have given you Andrew himself."

"But you did. He was here with us this morning. We could all feel his presence. And the gifts he gave us will be cherished for the rest of our lives. Thank you for making it possible. You are such an awesome brother, to Andrew as well as to me."

"You didn't always think that there have been times you would have gladly clobbered and disowned me," he said, chuckling.

"Well, that's true, but for now, you win the brother of the year award."

"Uncle James! Come see what my daddy gave me!" sounded from the living room.

"Go. I need to help Linda get this dinner going. I just want you to know that today *you're* my hero. Enjoy the status while you have it. Who knows what tomorrow will bring!"

"Wow, way to make a guy feel secure!" He gave her a fake punch in the arm and headed toward the living room.

Seven

The table was spread with what appeared to be enough food to feed an entire neighborhood. The mouth-watering aromas had been enticing everyone in the house for the last few hours, and at last they were going to enjoy the fruit of their labors.

As they paused for a moment and joined hands, Mary nodded to James. He cleared his throat and spoke softly, "Lord, You know best how difficult this year has been for all of us. But as we sit here today surrounded by this bounty, we are overcome with Your faithfulness. It is You who have brought us to this place. You have faithfully led us each step of the way, and You will faithfully walk with us through whatever the future holds. Today, we celebrate the greatest gift ever given to mankind—Jesus our Savior. May we never lose sight of Your great faithfulness to us, and may we remember that each of us is engraved forever in the palms of your hands.

"Thank you for this food now set before us and for the faithful hands that prepared it. May we use this nourishment to your glory and service. In Jesus's name we pray. Amen."

Echoing amens resounded around the table as the platters and bowls began to make their way around.

"How's that game of Scrabble going?" asked James.

"I think Matti has been studying the dictionary! But we're not done yet," said Colten.

"You're just mad because I got the word *parsimonious* on a double point square!"

"But who uses words like *parsimonious*! I bet you made it up and just got lucky. I bet it isn't even a real word!" said Colten.

"Actually, it means to be stingy or frugal to the extreme. I learned it in my English literature class. We were talking about the play 'The Christmas Carol,' and the teacher told us that Ebenezer Scrooge was parsimonious. Then, she made us look up the word to see what it meant. For some reason, the sound of it reminded me of persimmons, and it just stuck in my mind," said Matti.

James smiled, "Sounds like she has you there, son."

"Well, I'll get even with her after dinner," grumbled Colten, good-naturedly.

"This is great snow for a snowman, I think we need to go outside and play in the snow after dinner!" said Austin.

"Oh, that sounds like fun! We can make a snowman for each of us and have a whole snowman family," said Savannah.

"Savannah that would be eight snowmen. That's a lot of snow people. How about if we start with two or three and see how it goes?" asked Caitlyn.

"Okee-dokee. Besides, we might run out of snow if we make too many!" Savannah agreed.

The sound of Christmas music played softly in the living room as they continued the comfortable family banter. Mary was reminded again of how thankful she was for this family of hers.

After dinner, Matti and Caitlyn offered to do the dishes while Linda, James, and Mary retreated with coffee to the living room.

"Andrew would be very proud of his kids today," James observed as they relaxed in front of the crackling fireplace.

"I'm sure he would. I look back at the last year, and much of it seems a blur. I don't know how I got through it except to say the Lord was with me and had His hand on all of us. I am confident that He will never leave or forsake us, and that whatever lies ahead, He will continue to be faithful," Mary said.

"It is all He ever is. No matter how it may appear to us at the moment, He is always faithful. He never leaves us. It is we who sometimes choose to leave him for a time. But he never leaves us," added Linda.

"That reminds me of something," said Mary, chuckling softly. "One Sunday, when Caitlyn was only about two or so, I had to stop at the store after church for something. I don't like to shop on Sunday, but there was something I needed. Anyway, since I was just going to run in and get the one thing, I didn't get a cart. Now, you know how curious and impulsive Caitlyn was—"

"*Was?*" interrupted James, laughing.

"Well, you get the drift. Anyway, I didn't want to lose her in the store, but I wanted to have my hands free. So I said to her, 'Baby girl, I want you to hold on to Mommy's skirt and not let go. Whatever you do, do not let go of Mommy's skirt because I don't want to lose you.'"

"We hadn't been in that store for more than a minute when I noticed that something had captured her attention. I don't even remember what it was, but she was definitely intrigued with it. I could see the struggle going on inside her little head. She looked at her hand holding onto my skirt. Then, she looked at whatever it was that had caught her eye. Then, looking back at the hand holding my skirt, she suddenly dropped my skirt, reached down, and grabbed hold of her own dress and scooted across the store!"

The three of them laughed at the image and shook their heads. "That's our Caitlyn!" James said.

Mary continued, "The other day, I was remembering that incident, and the Lord spoke to my heart. He asked me if I had ever taken my eyes off Caitlyn, even when she scooted off on her own. And of course I answered Him, 'No, I didn't. She was my baby, and I wasn't about to take my eyes off her.'

"He responded by saying that, likewise, He never takes His eyes off of us, even when we leave him and take off on our own. He asked me what I did when she scampered off. Well, I followed her of course, took her hand, and brought her back to me."

"And His response to that?" asked Linda.

"He does the same with us. When we leave Him in pursuit of our own interests, He follows us, and if we will allow Him to, He will bring us back to Himself."

"It takes some of us longer than others to figure that out. How many times do we blame God for not caring about us when the problem is actually that we have left Him in pursuit of what the world hawks as important? If we would stand still for just a minute, we would notice that He is right behind us, watching and waiting for us to allow Him to take our hand and bring us back to Him," said James.

The room fell into a reflective silence as the fire popped in the fireplace. The three were enjoying the peace and comfort of just being together and the fellowship of their shared faith.

The silence was short lived, however, as suddenly they heard a whoop of laughter from the direction of the kitchen.

"Let's go finish up for the girls and send the children out to make those snowmen. "It will be dark soon, and we will have to be getting home," said Linda.

●　●　●

The house was quiet at last. The children were all fast asleep, and Mary sat watching the twinkling Christmas lights. Her hands closed around the warm cup of herbal tea as she re-lived the events of the day. The dinner had been fabulous, and Linda and James had spent the better part of the day with them. They had spoken to their parents and wished them Merry Christmas, and expressions of love had been exchanged all around. It had turned out to be a very snowy Christmas, so it was good they hadn't tried to travel over the pass.

The children had played in the snow until they were done in. They made snowmen and a snow fort, from which they conducted snow wars. It was good to see the older children really let down and act like children again. *They are growing up way too fast,* she thought. Late in the afternoon, the children had coerced the adults into joining them in a game of "Fox and Geese." Mary had forgotten the magic and joy of simply playing in the snow!

Afterward they all convened to the kitchen for hot chocolate and pumpkin pie. Mary had instructed the younger children to brush their teeth and put on their pajamas before they retired to the living room. The Christmas Story was playing on television, and they all snuggled down to watch it. Before it was half over, Savannah and Austin were fast asleep. The rest of them all laughed and enjoyed the movie as much as the first time they watched it.

All too soon the day was over. Linda, James, and two, sleepy kids packed themselves and a box of leftovers into the van and headed home.

Mary had a little time alone with Caitlyn before she sent her to bed, too. It was easy to forget that Caitlyn was, in many ways, still a little girl. Today's world tried to encourage girls to grow up way too fast. Why, Mary was still playing with dolls at thirteen years old! Thirteen was a hard age—one day you wanted to be treated like an adult, the next you wanted to be sheltered and protected as if you were still a child. Everyone around you noticed the mood changes and wanted you to shape up. And you would if you could, but the truth is, most thirteen year olds are just as confused by the way they feel as others are confused by the way they act. So Mary tried to stay tuned in to Caitlyn and what she might be going through. Not that she always felt successful, but Caitlyn was certainly worth the effort, and she would continue to do her best, and be thankful for the Lord's guidance.

It had been good to just sit and snuggle with Caitlyn and talk about the day, their feelings, and life in general.

The next day might bring another war of wills, but that night they were just mom and daughter enjoying the glow of Christmas and the love they had for one another.

Mary sighed heavily. Over the last two days, her emotions had been all over the map, and the result was pure exhaustion. However, she felt a sense of peace and something akin to contentment. She wondered if she would ever feel complete contentment again without Andrew, but time would tell. She knew time was a great healer and so was her Savior, so she would continue to rest in Him. *Or at least try to between bouts of severe panic,* she thought wryly.

As she fingered her charm bracelet and the little bumblebee charm, she smiled. *Andrew, you were always the best at planning surprises, but you really outdid yourself this time,* she thought. The children hadn't been able to stop talking about the gifts from their daddy. Here she had been so worried about not having gifts for them, but the Lord had it covered, all along. She reflected on the Word, which tells us that God knows our needs before we even ask. Would she ever learn to turn to Him *before* she set herself off into a dither? She hoped so. In the meantime, she would remain thankful for the Lord's never-ending faithfulness to her, even when she was in a dither.

She suppressed a yawn and looked at her watch. It was late, and she needed to be up and at work early tomorrow. It would be another short night for her. She took her cup to the kitchen and placed it in the sink. She hated to leave the children alone this week while they were out of school, but she didn't have the money for a babysitter. Besides, she was babysitting other people's children when she was Caitlyn's age, and they had Miss Elsie next door to look in on them from time to time. Miss Elsie was an elderly widow who lived next door. She had come to Mary's rescue on more than one occasion when she had not been able to get home before the children did. She didn't know what she would have done without her in the weeks following Andrew's death.

Miss Elsie loved the children and worried over them as if they were her own grandchildren. And the children loved her and tried to look after her in return. There were no fences between the two houses, only a drive, so the children often ran back and forth in both yards while they played. Miss Elsie would sit on her front porch and watch them or converse with them while she tended the flowers around her house. It was a comfort to know she was there if the children needed her.

As she walked through the house turning the lights off, Mary asked the Lord to energize her and give her wisdom for the coming days. She knew it would be a busy week helping Grace with all of her holiday meetings and parties. She prayed that the Lord would reveal himself to Grace in such a way that Grace would receive Him. Grace's life seemed so very shallow, consumed with possessions and status among her peers. And poor little Jack seemed to get lost in the shuffle. He was a darling little boy who wanted nothing more than to be loved and noticed by his parents.

Jack had every material possession one could imagine for a five-year-old boy, but he showed no interest in most of it. He spent a lot of time tagging behind Mary, even though Grace discouraged such interaction. She hired a nanny to care for Jack, but although the nanny tended his basic needs and could never be accused of being negligent, she seemed to lack the ability to relate to Jack as a real, little person.

Mary wondered how Jack had spent his Christmas day. She hoped Grace and Mark had found it in themselves to put aside their ambition and aspirations long enough to just be a family with Jack for the day.

Her last thoughts as she drifted off to sleep were of Andrew and the many Christmases they had spent together. What a wealth of memories…

Eight

The next morning, just before eight o'clock, Mary let herself in the back door. The huge kitchen, all stainless steel and granite, was a bit cluttered but wasn't as bad as Mary had expected. She set her purse in the butler's pantry and was removing her coat when Jack burst into the room.

"Mary, guess what I got for Christmas!" Before Mary could answer, he continued, "A uncle!"

Mary heard laughter in the hall, and Grace swept in after Jack. Mary was surprised to see Grace wearing jeans and a sweatshirt, and in her stocking feet. Her beautiful features were without makeup, and her hair was pulled up in a ponytail. It was surprise enough to witness Grace in such a casual state, but what happened next made her jaw drop in surprise.

"Jack, you come back here, you little urchin!" Grace laughed as she scooped Jack up in a bear hug. "Mary just got here. Give her a minute to put her things down."

To Mary's continued astonishment, Grace then turned to her and said," Mary, why don't you pour yourself a cup of coffee and come into the living room. I have someone I want you to meet and some things to discuss with you."

Doing a mental headshake, Mary did as Grace suggested. She left her coat in the kitchen and followed Grace and Jack into the living room.

As she entered the room, Mary wondered if she was dreaming. *Am I having one of those dreams where you dream you got up and have started your day, when in fact you are still asleep?* she thought to herself. The room was... well, it looked like a normal family living room the day after Christmas! With the exception of the fact that it was twice the size of a normal living room and three times more elegant, that is. There was wrapping paper and ribbon scattered about the room, and little boy toys and treasures were deposited throughout.

Grace had always been a stickler for all things pertaining to children being contained to the nursery. Her motto had been, "The living room is the first thing people see when they are welcomed into the house. It will be their first impression of us and must at all times be impeccably presentable." Mary thought it ironic that Grace seldom referred to the house as a home—but rather a house. However, today it felt like a home. *What happened?* she wondered.

Grace interrupted her thoughts. "Mary, I would like you to meet my uncle. Uncle, this is Mary, our housekeeper, although, she is so much more to us than a housekeeper. She keeps us grounded, and I don't know what we would do without her."

Mary smiled and said hello to a pleasant looking gentleman looking to be in his mid-fifties. He stood and shook her hand. There was something about him that seemed vaguely familiar, but before she could ask him anything, Grace continued.

"Please have a seat and make yourself comfortable." Grace perched on the edge of the small sofa across from her. "I need to ask you to forgive me. I'm afraid I have shamelessly taken advantage of you in the past. I want you to know, that is going to change—beginning today. You see, I sort of lost my way for a while, but well, I think I have found my way back."

Mary settled herself in the overstuffed chair and waited. Grace looked down briefly but then took a deep breath and settled back in her chair before continuing.

"A few years ago, I went through a time of great personal loss. I lost both of my parents to cancer within a year. A year before that, my only other living relative, my dad's brother, disappeared from our lives. I didn't know where he was or how to reach him. I think I just built a wall around my heart and refused to feel anything because it seemed safer than loving and losing those you loved. I turned my back on my faith and my God. It's sad to say, but even having Jack did not thaw the frozen, barren landscape of my heart.

Jack reached up and cupped Grace's face in his two little hands. "Don't be sad, Mommy." Grace gave him a hug in response.

"Mommy isn't sad, honey. Mommy is just telling Miss Mary a story. Can you listen while Mommy finishes her story?"

"Does the story end good?" Jack asked softly.

"Yes, dearest, it ends very good."

"Okay." Jack said, and snuggled into Grace's lap.

She continued, "I thought I could fill the void with possessions and stature in the community, but those things only perpetuated more grasping and grabbing for that elusive something that promised to fill the empty places—but never did. It even began to affect my marriage. Mark could tell how empty I was, and the harder he tried to fill the emptiness, the more I pushed him away. He even went back to church and begged me to go with him. He said he was learning to trust in God for his own peace, and he told me I would never find the peace I am seeking without the Lord, but I refused to go with him.

Her coffee forgotten, Mary leaned forward in her chair.

Andrew's Gift

"As you know, we had a party here on Christmas Eve. Actually, Mark didn't want to have it. He wanted us to go to church, but I insisted and he finally gave in. From a social perspective, the party was a big hit. I should have been satisfied, but for some reason it left me feeling more empty and lonely than ever before." She paused. "Mary, have you been praying for me?"

Mary just smiled and nodded.

"Well, between you and Mark, your prayers have been answered. After that party, I had what my granny used to call a 'come to Jesus meeting.' I sat in front of this tree and finally poured my heart out to God. I won't go into the details, but suffice it to say, God and I had a lot of unfinished business to take care of. I didn't know that I had that many tears in me! Isn't there a verse some place that says God actually saves our tears? Oh, Mary! When I think of the tears you must have shed this past year... And I was so self-involved that I was no support to you at all! I am so ashamed of myself now. I will never be able to make it up to you, but I am certainly going to try."

"We both are going to try."

Mary looked up as Mark walked into the room. Mark was a good-looking young man—tall and slender. He had a casual, loose-jointed way of walking that belayed the fact that he was a wise and shrewd businessman. Mark walked over and sat next to Grace. He kissed her on the cheek and took her hand. Jack bolted from Grace's lap and landed in Mark's. "Daddy! Did you finish your business stuff?"

"Yes, buddy, I did." He looked apologetically at Mary. "I'm sorry for interrupting. I have been canceling appointments. Grace and I are both taking the rest of the holidays off to concentrate on our home and family. We both want you to be able to do the same with yours, Mary. But I'm getting ahead of Grace's story. Jack, buddy, let's be polite and let Mommy talk now."

Grace smiled and ruffled Jack's hair. "I love you, Jack. Can you sit quietly here, or do you need to go play?"

Jack thought about it for a minute. "I can sit quietly, Mommy. I like being with you and Daddy."

Hugging Jack again, Grace continued, "After taking care of business with God on Christmas Eve, I awoke on Christmas morning feeling more alive than I can ever remember feeling. I couldn't wait to celebrate the birth of Christ as a family. I wanted to tell Jack the story of the first Christmas, and I was ashamed that he had never heard it from us before. We had a wonderful time with him, explaining what Christmas was really about, and we were just sitting down to watch him open his gifts when the doorbell rang. I opened the door to find a stranger standing on my doorstep, or at least someone I thought to be a stranger. He looked like a street person, and I thought he was asking for a handout. But when he spoke I knew the voice. After being gone for five years, my uncle was standing at my door."

Mary turned to acknowledge the gentleman who had been sitting quietly by the fire the whole time.

"His story isn't mine to tell, but let me just say that he has been through a hard time, too, the last several years, and we have a lot of catching up to do. Why, Jack wasn't even born yet the last time we saw him.

"So, as you might imagine, what a Christmas we had yesterday! Mary, for the first time in years, I started to feel alive. And as the glacier I had built around my heart began to melt, I began to look at my life through new eyes. I saw how God has truly blessed me in spite of my selfishness and bitterness, and I saw how I had allowed my bitterness to dictate how I treated others—including you. This is Christmas break, and your children are home without their mother because of my selfishness."

Grace rose and walked over to a small desk in the corner of the room. From the drawer, she retrieved an envelope. She then returned to sit next to Mary.

"Here is the bonus I promised you before Christmas. I am ashamed of myself for being so self-involved that I didn't consider how my broken promise might affect your Christmas plans. Mary, can you ever forgive me?"

Mary smiled and said, "It's already done, Grace. I *do* forgive you."

Before she could say more, Grace continued, "That's not all, Mary. When we are finished talking, I want you to go home and spend the Christmas break with your children—with full pay."

Mary was dumbfounded. "But… but what about your women's group and your meetings?"

Grace held up her hand. "I'm not done yet. We have more cars in our garage than we can ever drive at one time. I have called our insurance agent and, as of today, you are insured to drive any of our vehicles. As long as you are working for me, you will have a car at all times. In the envelope along with your bonus is the information you will need to access our account at the gas station indicated. Just go there and keep the gas tank full at our expense. That includes gas for your personal use.

"Now, concerning the women's group and various meetings, I have rescheduled all of them until after the holidays. You aren't the only one with family, you know," she said good-naturedly. "I have a lot of time to make-up with all three of the men in my life. Jack is home from school, and I intend to make the most of that time. Mark has been patient for a long time, waiting to get his wife back. And now I have my uncle back. I think if I get any happier, I will simply burst!"

"Ka-Plow!" exclaimed Jack. They all started and looked at him in alarm. "I'm happier than you, Mommy, and I just 'burst.' Ka-Plow! I burst again!"

"You can always trust a child to bring comic relief," Grace's uncle spoke for the first time.

They all laughed in agreement.

Mary turned to look again at Grace's uncle. He smiled and shifted in his seat. As he did, the light caught a flash of gold on his lapel. Mary's breath caught in her throat, and she stammered, "G... Grace, I didn't catch your uncle's name."

He smiled again and responded. "I'm sorry. In the excitement of your arrival, we forgot. To Grace, I've always been simply, 'Uncle.' Mary, my name is Max, and it is my pleasure to make your acquaintance."

"It's nice to meet you Max. Um, I'm sorry if I sound nosey, but, um, may I ask where you got that little gold pin on your lapel?"

"You may ask indeed. God gave it to me. His messenger was an angel. An angel named Savannah. You see, God doesn't only use children for comic relief. It is through the mouths of babes that we often receive God's most profound lessons. Did you know, Mary that the bumblebee should not be able to fly? It shouldn't, but it does. Just like the bumblebee, life sometimes doesn't make sense to us humans. But if we will put our trust in God, we will learn that He can use those things in our lives to teach us to fly. After running from God and from life for five years, the words of a little girl and her gift to me of this pin opened the eyes of this old sinner." He touched the pin gently. Tears were now flowing freely down his cheeks. "What I didn't even tell Grace is that I was going to end it all that night. It was Christmas Eve, just five years ago that night that I lost my wife and daughter. I just couldn't bear to live any longer with the pain of losing them. That dinner was going to be, as it were, my last supper."

"Oh, Uncle!" Grace walked over and embraced her uncle. The tears were flowing down her cheeks, as well. "I am so glad you came home instead! You are the best Christmas gift, next to Jesus, that I have ever received! That little angel will never know the end of the story, but I hope God will bless her for her act of love to you! God is so incredibly faithful."

You don't know the half of it! thought Mary to herself. *What an awesome God we serve! Only God can see how so many lives were intertwined, and bring this puzzle together!* She thought of the bumblebee; *it shouldn't be able to fly, but it did. With God, all things are possible!*

"Mary?"

Mary looked up and replied, "Yes?"

Grace looked at her quizzically. "You said, 'You don't know the half of it.' What do you mean?"

"Oh! Did I say that out loud? "Mary laughed through her own tears. "I didn't realize I said it out loud. I was thinking to myself."

"So can you share the 'half of it,' or is it personal?" continued Grace.

"I would love to share it with you," Mary smiled and wiped her tears. "Make yourselves comfortable."

• • •

As Mary drove home, her emotions and thoughts were all jumbled. By the time she had finished telling her side of the story, they were all in tears. And before she left, they all joined hands in a prayer of thanksgiving for God's incredible faithfulness. Then, Grace, Mark, and Max insisted on setting a day during the school break for Mary to bring the children to the house. "It is a crying shame that your children and Jack have never met, and he would dearly love to have new playmates!"

"Yes! I want to show them my room, and we can make a snow fort in the back yard!" said Jack.

"See there? It's settled. We'll plan lunch and let the children get to know each other," said Grace.

"And I can see my little angel again," added Max

Mary's mind drifted, as it so often did, to thoughts of Andrew. Pictures, like a kaleidoscope, flashed through her mind: Andrew changing the oil in Miss Elsie's car, Andrew shoveling snow at the church before Sunday service, Andrew playing basketball with the boys at the boys' club, and Andrew talking to the children about the value of helping others. But he didn't just tell them; he showed them by his example. And whenever he could, he would take at least one of the children with him. He said he got more bang out of his buck that way. Not only did he get to help someone who had a need, but he got to spend time with his children at the same time.

People were always telling her that Andrew had the gift of helping others. But as she thought about it, something occurred to her. Andrew didn't *have* a gift—he *was* the gift. Andrew's gift to the world around him, to his family and ultimately to his country, was himself. And, like ripples in a pond, the gift he gave would keep giving. His children were proof of that by the way they chose to help others on Christmas Eve instead of receiving gifts for themselves.

The children will be so excited to see her and know that she will be home with them for their whole Christmas break! She had mentally done the math and thought that after putting some of her bonus money in the bank for emergencies, she could take the children out for an after-Christmas shopping trip. There were a few things they really needed, and it would be fun to let them pick them out themselves.

As she drove into her own driveway, three little heads appeared in the brightly lit window. She breathed a sigh of gratitude and contentment. "Thank You, Lord, for Your awesome provision and faithfulness. The New Year does indeed hold the promise of a new beginning for us. And with your help, we will learn to fly, Lord. We *will* learn to fly."

She got out of the car and started up the walk, laughing out loud at the surprised looks on the faces of her children. *My dear, beautiful children,* she thought, *you don't know the half of it...*

Christmas Heart

I've re-arranged the furniture to make room for the tree
I've re-arranged the pantry for my annual baking spree
I've re-arranged my schedule to shop and bake and sew
I've re-arranged the outdoor tools, hoping for some snow

• • •

But before I do another thing, before I let the season start
In the quiet of this moment Lord, please rearrange my
heart

• • •

Oh, precious, holy Father, You gave Your only Son
That we could have eternal life through Him, the Holy
One
And though Your gift cannot be matched or placed beneath
a tree
Let me give what's not convenient, let me give a part of me
Your gift cannot be purchased, yet its value has no end
So let my gift be priceless, let me pause and be a friend

• • •

As You sent Your gift to us that night, in form of infant
man
Let me see this holy story through a child's eyes once again

May the wonder and the glory pour through everything I
do
With the excitement of a child let my heart be filled with
You

      ●   ●   ●

Then let the Christmas banner of the Lord be lifted high
I will deck the halls, pray for snow, and bake a pumpkin pie
I will fill my home with wondrous smells, I'll decorate the
tree
But let the world see Christ in Christmas, and let it start
with me